YAARI

Presented by- Bshayar52

COMPILED BY :-SAMPURNA MISHRA

DISCLAIMER

This is a work of fiction. Our editors have tried their best to edit the content of all the author/authors and check the plagiarism. All the write-ups in this book are unique and are only published in this book. In case any plagiarism or error is found, the author is the sole responsible and not the publisher

Presented by- Bshayar52

"Yaari"
By: Ms. Sampurna Mishra
Presented by: Bshayar52
ISBN: 978-81-948258-9-0
Fiction 1st Edition
Book Editor: Mr.Rudra Narayan Sahu
Cover Design: Mr.Arijit Das

ACKNOWLEDGEMENTS

First and foremost, I would like to thank my parents, without whom, I wouldn't be here.

In the process of putting this book together, I realized how much effort had gone into each book that I've read before. It has been an immense pleasure working hard for my first anthology.

I would also like to express my gratitude towards BSHAYAR52 which provided us this platform, to all writers to touch the heights of their dreams.

I would also like to extend a sincere thanks to all my co-writers for actively supporting me through this journey. I would not have been to successfully compile this book without their active and constant help.

At the end, I would like to thank all my readers who have understood me, and have believed in me.

INTRODUCTION

The feeling of friendship and the word friend it's like music to ears. As said by aristotle, "man is a social animal". Yes indeed we are , we are greedy of love and affection. We as a human being search for a helping hand in this world of strangers. Friends comes to us for rescue in such a situation. They are our life time therapists and comedians. They are what we search for in everyone , just someone to say " hey, do u want to be my friend?"

Shahnoor Shaikh

Shahnoor Shaikh was born on 2-02-2001 in Mumbai.Who is currently pursuing D-phrm (1st year) She is young & talented with her god grace skills for writing books. She has innumerable fann following on social media platform (Insta blog @beintehaa_ishq -"aashiqana andaz'' This tiny Girl aims to inspire people through her writing and wanted to spread Love & Happiness forever!! Let's cherish with the dynamic personality who aims to win all hearts.

Dosti me Pyaar.

Nafrat Hai Pyaar Se, Ishq Hai Mere Yaar Se.
Teri Aur Meri Yaari,
Duniya Me Hai Sabse Pyaari.
Tu Hi Meri Aan, Tu Hi Meri Shan
Zindagi Ki Sari Khushiya Aye Dost Tujh Pe Qurbaan.
Jo Same Par Saath Nahi Chorta Hai, Wo Hi Asal Me Saccha Dost Hota Hai.
Pyaar Me Kuch Junoon Sa Hai, Dosti Me Sara Sukoon Sa hai.
Fark Logo Ki Nazar Me Hai,
Warna Dosti Bhi Pyaar Se Kam Nahi Hai

Dosti sabse khaas

Tu Hi Mera Pyaar, Tu Hi Mera Yaar Tere Bin Aadhura Lage Ye Sara Sansaar.

Ye Jo Mera Yaar Hai, Bahut Hi Khas Hai.

Izzat Doge Izzat Paoge, Warna Mere Dost Ke Dande Khaoge. Sabko Apni Dosti Par Guroor Hai, Mere Dost Bhi Kohinoor Hai.

Khoon ke Riste Se Badh Kar Hamara Rista Hai, Tu Hi meri zindagi ka Special Hissa Hai.

Haath Ki Lakeeron Me Kuch To Baat Hai, Is Liye Aap Jaisa Dost Hamare Paas Hai.

Na Jane Kismat Ne Kaise Mila Diya Hame, Anjaan Chahere Ko Khas Dost Bana Diya Rab Ne.

Natkhat Pyaar

I Love You Jaani,

Tu Hai Meri Zindagi Ki Kahani.

Apni Zindagi Ki Nawab Hu Mein, Teri Dosti Me Badnaam Hu Mein.

Chal Hat Chal Bhak,Tu Mera Yaar Hai Duniya Me Bas.

Yaha Kadam Kadam Par Fankaar Milte Hai, Sache Dost Har Kismat Walon Ko Milte Hai.

Dosti Me Dost Hamara Khuda Sa Hota Hai, Mehsoos Tab Hota Hai Jab Wo Juda Hota Hai.

Wafa Itni Karo Kabhi Bewafayi Na Bane, Dosti Aisi Karo Kabhi Judayi Na Bane.

Dost Teri Dosti Bhi Qubool Hai, Zindagi Me Teri bhul bhi Ek phool Hai.

Aye Dost Is Dosti Me Hum Juda Ho Jaye, Isse Accha Hai Hum Pehle Hi Fana Ho Jaaye

Dost Ki Yaad Kuch Tujh Pe Udhar Hai, Kuch Mujh Pe Udhar Hai Dosti Ki Ye Mithi Yaaden

Ek Baar Milne Ki Tarasdaar Hai.

Aye Dost Mana Ki Fursat Nahi tujhe Meko Yaad Karne Ki, Par Mera Dil Nhi Manta Tujhe Khas Se Aam Karne Ki.

Hamari Thodi Mazboori Hai, Aye Dost Is Liye Doori Hai.

Waise To Laakho Mil Jaye,

Par Jab Tu Mile Tab Jeene Ki Wajah Mil Jaye.

Aye Dost Hum Tumhe Hamesha Yaad Karte Hai, Rab Se Hamesha Milne Ki Fariyaad Karte Hai.

Aye Dost Door Ho To Baat Kar Liya Karo, Shant Reh Kar Hame Saza Na Diya Karo

Dosti hai jaan

Nazar Na Lage Is Riste Ko Zamane Ki, Meri Bhi Tammanna Hai Is Dosti Ko Maut Tak Nibhane Ki.

Dost Karti Hu Aap Se Behad Pyaar, Ab Banalo Mujhe Apna Yaar.

Ek Hasti Hai Jo Meri Shan Hai, Mere Dost Ko Mera Salam Hai

Aapki Dosti Ne Hame Jeena Sikha Diya, Rote Huye Dil Ko Hansna Sikha Diya.

Dosti Ne Hamari Ek Mode Liya hai, Mode Ne Hame Ek Dusre Se Jod Diya hai

Zindagi Me Dosti Hai Hame Pyaari, Dost Ke Liye Hai Hazir Jaan Hamari.

Meri Ek Dost Bahut Khas Hai, Jo Mere Jigar Ke Pass Hai.

Tu Hi Meri Duniya Aur Tu Hi Meri Jaan Hai, Tere Bina Ye Zindagi Ek Wiraan Hai.

Anuradha Gupta
"Electrical Engineer"

It is not easy to write your feelings but I like to write

She is pursuing diploma with electrical branch.Her college is V. J. B. Government girl's polytechnic Jhansi

DOST BHUT AATE HAI ZINDAGI ME

Khne ko to bhut dost mile zindagi me Magar tere jaesa yarr na mila, Zindagi me bhut aate h dosti krne ko Magar tere jaesa dost na mila,

Dosti me samjate to sabhi hai

Magar tere jaesa samjne wala yar na mila, Apne gum sub btane aate hai mujhe Magar mujhe sunne wala tere jaesa

Koi aur yar na mila,

Sub khash bnne aate hai zindagi me Magar aam bnke rh jate hai,

Ek tu h jo aam bnne aaya tha Or mera khash bn kr rh gaya...

 BEST FRIEND FOREVER

DOSTI SUCHCHI HAI

Wo mere liye suraj ki tarah hai,
Meri zindagi me roshni uske hone se hai,
Agar mujhe koi takleef ho to dhuk use bhi hota hai,
Wo mere dard ko mahsus kr leta hai
Khne ko to wo kuch dikhata he nahi Bs andar he andar
bate rakh leta hai,
Wo meri khushiyon ka khayal kuch Ese rkhta hai,
Ki Mere mangne se phle meri har Murad puri kr krta
hai,
Mere zindagi me *dost*
Esa diya khuda ne jo hmesha Meri galtiyon pr bhi pyar
se samja Diya krta hai...
Love u yara

PURANE YARO SE, YAARI

Me khash bhut thi tere liye
Or shayad aaj bhi khash hu na, Galti kuch meri thi to
Kuch galti ki bjah tu bhi hai na,
Hm Sath nahi hai to koi gila nahi Chalo fir Milne ka
kbhi socho na, Hm dur dur to bhut rh liye
Kbhi pass aane ka socho na,
Kahi tu bhi pareshan hai zindagi se Or kahi me bhi
preshan hu logo se Chal dono ki pareshaaniyon
Ko dur krne ka kbhi socho na
Ab manane ka riwaj nahi raha To ab Purani bato ko
chhodo na,
Dono ko bhut yar mil liye zindagi me Ab in sub ki yari
ko chhod kr
Purani yari ke bare me kbhi socho na,
Kbhi hmne bhi sath rhne ki Kasmein khayi thi
Fir unke he vaste kbhi apni Dosti ka bhi socha na....

DOST TU KHASH HAI

Tujhse milne ke phle kuch nahi tha Zindagi me,
Tere aane se khush rhna shikha Hai mene,
Tera meri zindagi me hona he bhut hai Tere na hone se
kuch bhi nahi hu me, Tujhse he meri sari khushi hai
Tu he meri har problam ka solution hai, Ese he tujhe me
bestie nahi khti
Tu hai is kabil ki har bat me tujhse khti
Tu samajta hai mujhe tbhi to me hu Tere sath
Varna ese he nahi hai tu mera khas...

HOSTEL WALI YAARI

Kuch ko jigri yar mile,

Kuch ko dhokhebaaj yr mile, Kisi ne ek dost ke khatir subko chhod diya,

Or kisi ne subke liye

ek achcha dost chhod diya,

Kisi ko zindagi bhar ka yar mila, Or kisi ko jhuta pyar mila,

Subne milkr rhne ki kasmein khayi thi, Aaj kon kon sath hai

Ye subne aazmayi thi, Aaj teen saal ho gaye Hm sub dur ho gaye,

Na jane kb milne ki bari aayegi, Na jane kb gumo ki bhar jayegi, Wo holi me gulal lagana

Or subko pani me bhigana, Or mitti me subko lita ke Usko mitti lagana,

Or bad me usko pani se nahlana,

Yade subki hai

Mulakate subki hai Din yad rhta hai Saal yad rhti hai

Or yad rhta h afsaana... Missing you yaro

Abbas manager

Abbas Manager, 20 year old residing in ujjain, Madhya Pradesh, is studying Bcom, and also running a business hereafter. He is an ambivert writer of his eternal emotions and loves being childish at times

यार अनमोल

कुछ रिश्ते अपने आप बनते है!
कोई और नहीं,हम खुद उन्हें चुनते है!!
ज़िन्दगी के हर सुख और दुख में उनका साथ होता है!
वो सबसे पहले हर रिश्ता उनके बाद होता है!!
दोस्ती जितनी पुरानी उतनी लाजवाब होता है!
जैसे बंद बॉटल में हर कटरा शराब होती है!!
चलते है हमकदम,हमराह,हर मोड़ पर!
जाट पात, उंच नीच, सारी बंधिशो को तोड कर!!
दोस्तो में दूरी हो, तो दिल बेताब होता है!
दोस्त तो हमारे बचपन कि खुली किताब होता है!!
बचपन से जवानी तक यही हमारे साथ होते है!
तारो की गर्दिश में दोस्त आफताब होते है!!
जिसको तुम्हारी हर बात से ऐतराज़ रहे!
गम ना करना अगर वो हमराज़ ना रहे!!
बिना सोचे कह सको दिल की बातें जिसको!
कुछ ना होकर भी वो शख़्स एहसास में रहे!!
रविय्या बदलने पर छोर जाए जो ज़माना तो गम ना कर!
बिना देखे जो खामोशी समझले यार ऐसा तलाश कर!

Best friends:- irritating yet support

Friends like you are hard to find... Genuinely caring and purely kind... My love for you is i wish to say....
Like planets floating in the milky way...
With you i have spend my childhood days We have enjoyed life in many ways..
I cant thank you for the support you give.. Forever i wish together live....
Surely with time our friendship has taken a mile..
But thank you for making me laugh even when i dont want to smile No matter how angry you get on me and shout..
But only you walk in when for me,when the rest of the world walk out..
Our friendship cant be defined with a particular name..
You are like a gold ring with rarest gem..
I wish our friendship last long...
So we can walk miles forever along..

बचपन के दोस्त

बचपन की दोस्ती का हर दिन अनमोल है!
मेरे हर fever का तू paracetamol hai!!
तेरे साथ गुजरा हर वक़्त याद आता है!
तू पास क्यों नहीं मेरे, ये खयाल मुझे सताता है!!

जब जब में गिरता हूं, तुम मुझे उठाते हो!
गलती करने पर हमेशा मुझे समझते हो!!
मूड अच्छा ना होने पर, तुम मुझे हसाते हो!
मेरे मन को सबसे ज़्यादा तुम बहलाते हो!!

माना के आजकल सब पर ज़िम्मेदारियों का बोलबाला है!
मगर दोस्ती ने ज़िन्दगी को बड़ी खूबसूरती से संभाला है!!
मेरे हर गम को वो अपना मानता है!
मेरे अल्फ़ाज़ से ज़्यादा, वो मेरी खामोशी को जानता है!!

Unexpected friends:- Far away but close to heart

Unexpected friendship's are the best....

These friends are different from rest...

Slowly they becomes the part of ur life....

Just like the pair of fork and knife

One is useless.. other one is cute..

One is talkative and one is mute..

Uh are also one of that unexpected friend...

Who disturbs my day from starting to end...

Friends like uh are very rare...

Who gives a lot of importance and care.. With uh i can share my happiness and sorrow....

Whether its yesterday, today or tomorrow..

Uh are the person with whom i can laugh with...

For sure ur texts are annoying beneath

I pray uh may get the love of ur life...

Uh are Very desperate to become a wife Friends like uh remains deep inside the heart...

As uh are the defected piece of god's art

No love can take ur place my friend.. Be by my side till my end

दोस्तीः- एक एहसास

अनजान से जान होते है!
ज़िन्दगी की वो पहचान होते है!!
ज़िन्दगी के हर मोड़ पर जिनका साथ होता है!
रास्ते की हर ठोकर पर संभालने को इनका हाथ होता है!!

एक पैकेट मै 10-10 हाथ हुआ करते थे!
बचपन के दोस्त सब एक साथ हुआ करते थे!!
आजकल ज़िन्दगी की मश्रुफियत में मुलाकाते कुछ कम होती है!
मगर ये तो दोस्ती है जनाब ना मिलने से इसकी दौर कहा कमजोर होती है!!

परिवार से ज़्यादा दोस्त हमें जानते है!
हमारी हर तकलीफ और परेशानी को वो अपना मानते है!!
सच्चा दोस्त अगर मिल जाए तो वो खुदा से कम नहीं!
फिर चाहे छोर भी जाए अगर ज़माना तो कोई ग़म नहीं!

Sagar jain

He is jain sagar from Mumbai 37, programming student by profession and writer and singer by passion,loves to learn new things, he is the personality who always believes in only karma,wants to make smile on everyone's face by my writeups and good deeds.

सहारा लेता हूं दिल के जज्बातों को बयां करने के लिए कागज और कलम का..

लिखता वहीं हूं जो दिल कहता है और जिसे साथ नहीं है जुबां का।

बचपन वाली यारी

वो बचपन की दोस्ती भी क्या दोस्ती थी,

एक अगर नाव था तो दूसरा कश्ती थी।

अविस्मरणीय है कच्चे आम तोड़ने से लेकर साइकिल चलाने तक का सफर,

गिल्ली डंडा और क्रिकेट खेलने में रहते थे इतने मशगूल कि भूखे रहते थे पूरी दोपहर।

शाम को हुई लड़ाई को सुबह तक भूल जाते थे, और फिर अगली सुबह स्कूल का होमवर्क करने के लिए भी उसी के घर जाते थे।

खुद उसकी पतंग काट कर हंसना और दूसरे के काटने पर उसके साथ जुड़ जाना, उसकी मदद करना,

साथ-साथ नदी किनारे जाकर नहाना, हर वक्त साथ साथ ही रहना।

साथ स्कूल जाना ,एक साथ एक बैंच पर बैठना और फिर रिसेस में एक दूसरे का टिफिन खाना,

किसी ने मुझे या फिर उसे किसी ने तंग किया तो मास्टरजी के पास जाकर शिकायत करना और उसे डांट खाते हुए छुप-छुपकर हंसना।

होली पर उसे गुजिया खिलाना और ईद पर उसके शिरकुरमा खाना, दिवाली पर साथ-साथ पटाखे फोड़ना और क्रिसमस पर चर्च जाकर कैंडल जलाना।

बदला वक्त ,बदला जमाना, बदले आखिर लोग भी ,नहीं बदली तो सिर्फ वो यारी हमारी,

बदल सकते हैं चांद और सूरज, पृथ्वी भी एक दिन, पर नहीं बदलेगी
तो सिर्फ वो यारी हमारी।
कभी ना दुखे दिल उसका, न उस पर कोई संकट आए,
यारा तेरी और मेरी यारी दुनिया के लिए मिसाल बन जाए।।

याराना

हर मुश्किल लगती है आसान ,जब होता है हम यारों को एक- दूसरे का साथ।

उनके चेहरे की हंसी और मुस्कान को देख कर भी दिल को मिलता है बड़ा आराम।

किया है यारों ने आज तक यारों की हर महफिल में हमें हमेशा शरिक,

ऐसे यार हैं हम और यारी हमारी कि आज तक वो महफिल नहीं हुई जिस महफिल में हम ना हुए हो शरिक।

कुछ तो खास बात है इस दोस्ती के रिश्ते में..

साथ इनके होने से हमेशा आ जाती है मुझमें हिम्मत,

मजबूत हो जाते हैं इरादे सारे ,जो दिखा दे अगर मुझे कोई आंख तो फिर आ जाती है उसकी शामत।

मंजिल दूर होकर भी जीतने का एहसास दिलाती है दोस्ती,

जीते-जी जन्नत का एहसास कराती है दोस्ती।

अपनी हर उलझन का हल पाने के लिए आ जाता है मेरे पास दौड़ा भागा,

एक सच्चा साथी और हम दर्द पाया है मुझे मेरे उस यार ने अपनी नजरों में,

यार और दोस्त तो सिर्फ कहता है जुबां से, दिल से तो माना है उसने भाई- बंधु और सखा।

ऐ खुदा कभी वो दिन ना लाना, कभी ना आए आंसू उसकी आंखों में, कभी ना गिराना मुझे उसकी नजरों में।

तुम्हारी मेरी यारी

बेशक शरारती और नटखट है सब के सब पर उनके होने से ही है सुकुन,

साथ देते हैं मेरा सदा चाहें तकलीफ हो दर्द।

नहीं पता चलता है इनके साथ होने से वक्त का पता,

होते हैं जब साथ मेरे , मेरे यार, कह पड़ता है वक्त भी मुझसे जी ले अपनी जिंदगी।

न नाराज होने देते हैं, न रूठने देते हैं और फिर भी रूठ जाऊं तो थप्पड़ लगा देते हैं,

रोते हुए भी हंसा देते हैं और फिर भी रो दूं तो गले से लगा लेते हैं।

देखा है मैंने ,मुझे तकलीफ में देखकर उन्हें मायूस होते हुए,

उस मायुसियत को पीछे छोड़, डटकर सामना करते हुए मुझे जीताते हुए।

सिखाया है यारी ने हीं हमें खुद की परवाह ना कर, यारों को बचाना, उनके लिए किसी से भी लड़ जाना,

मुश्किल वक्त में भी लोटपोट कर हंसना और मुसीबत को मात दे देना।

किसी विशेष दिन की जरूरत नहीं पड़ती हमें पार्टी करने के लिए,

यारों के साथ टपरी पर बैठकर चाय पीना और सड़क किनारे की पानी पुरी भी कोई पार्टी से कम नहीं होती।

यार तो सभी पाते हैं, मैंने भी पाए हैं यार,

पर मैंने औरों से कुछ अलग पाए हैं यार।

कौन कहता है कि धरती पर स्वर्ग नहीं है,

मैंने मेरे यारों के साथ बिताया हर एक लम्हा स्वर्ग के समान पाया है।

वो चार यार

एक गहरा सा रिश्ता जुड़ जाता है इन यारों से,

कुछ अपने से, जान से लगने लगते हैं, लगाव हो जाता है इन यारों से।

कुछ खट्टी सी, मीठी सी और प्यार की नोक झोंक वाली यारी है हमारी,

जान बुझकर खुद का मजाक बनाकर यारों के चेहरे पर हंसी लाने की कोशिश करने वाली यारी है हमारी।

जिया है हर लमहे को, जो बिताया है मैंने मेरे यारों के साथ, खुलकर,

जिंदगी में पल नहीं बल्कि पलों में जिंदगी को ढूंढ कर।

कमी को ताकत में बदलना बखूबी जानते हैं मेरे यार,

तैयार रहते हैं मेरे लिए हर घड़ी ,हर वक्त मेरे यार।

जिंदगी जीने का अंदाज सिखाती है दोस्ती,

बदलते वक्त के साथ हाथ थाम कर साथ चलना और नजरिया बदलना सिखाती है दोस्ती।

शान हो, मान हो, हो सम्मान तुम ,यारों जान हो तुम,

हूं मैं परिंदा अगर तो मेरे उड़ने के लिए खुला आसमान हो तुम।

जिंदगी जीने की छुपी हुई वजहो में से एक है दोस्ती,

कुछ अधूरी सी और बेरंग सी है जिंदगी, बिना दोस्त और दोस्ती।

दूरियां तो सिर्फ कहने की बात है ,है सिर्फ एक शब्द,

दूर रहकर भी पास होने का एहसास दिलाना, यारों के बारे में कुछ कहना या और यारी को दर्शाना है निशब्द।

एक तू ही यार मेरा

दोस्त तो बहुत बनें और मिलें,पर उस एक जैसा कोई नहीं,
कुछ तो खास बात है उस एक में, उसके जैसा दूजा कोई नहीं।

बिना कहें समझ लेता है सब कुछ वो मेरा यार,
हंसी के पीछे के दर्द और खामोशी के पीछे की वजह को भी ढूंढ लेता है वो मेरा यार।

जो बातें किसी से नहीं कह सकता या किसी को नहीं होती है पता,
वाकिफ हैं वो सारी खुशियों, गमों से,जानता है वो जिंदगी की सारी खता।

साथ रहा है हर वक्त,जब नहीं मिला मुझे किसी का साथ,
खड़ा रहा वो मेरे लिए, जूते की लेस खुलने से लेकर बांध लेने तक।

भाता है मन को मेरे,उसका चिढ़ाना , बचकानी हरकतें करना,बेवजह हंसना,
नाराज होने की संभावना और गुंजाइश तो नहीं है उसकी, फिर भी रूठ जाए अगर तो उसे मनाना।

यार नहीं रहा सिर्फ अब ,मान लिया है उसे भाई,बन गया है परिवार का एक हिस्सा,
याद है मुझे उसके साथ बिताये तमाम लम्हें, और उसका मेरा हर एक किस्सा।

माना कि सफर लंबा है जिंदगी का,कट जाएगा हंसते हसते,
नामुमकिन को मुमकिन में बदलेंगे हम यार मिलकर हंसते हंसते।

है याराना हमारा कुछ ऐसा कि जलते है कुछ लोग, तेरे साथ और
तेरी यारी के अलावा कुछ नहीं चाहिए,
ऐ यार अब जनम जनम यार के रूप में मुझे तू ही चाहिए।।

Linoka Chophi

Linoka Arsapa Chophi (2006-...) is a student with a pen name -linoka_Cx-. From Nagaland, Dimapur District Who got interested by reading poems written on her school books.

My beloved friends

'As sun rises up On a clear day'. "Shines upon me."
"Lights the path Into my future" 'Just as you,
The sun,
That shine upon me..
"People came and passed" Just like the clouds~ Floating
in the sky,
And kept throwing us apart...
But!!
The shine of your light , Shone so bright.
That kept the bond of 'Friendship' and 'Love'
Forever.

Happiness because of you

'Happiness' is a 'Peace of mind'
That people hinger for.
"Not knowing that Everything dont lasts
'Forever'.
'Depression takes place,' 'Sorrow holds,'
'Loosing hopes,'
But the pureness of friendship 'Empowers' and
'Overcomes' 'Motivation stands'
'Confidence takes place' 'Steps together',
And creates
The purest bond of 'friendship.'

Dear Friend

"Time passes so fast Not knowing how
You have been."
'Season changes', ' Years passes' "And my heart
Kept on missing you more And more.
 ~Wondering if we could spend like we We used to~.
You were the sun That lighted up my days!
And the stars
That twinkled upon me! "And through my rough days,
You stayed besides me.

Friendship according to me

"Friendship is a law that Never gets broken."
"Everytime it recreates itself 'Stronger'."
'That it reflects, beautifully like a diamond'
In the shape of a star 'With perfect edges'.
Cuts everything that tends to depart them.
~But smoothens that bonds Them~.

Friendship

'Friendship is a generation' With a road full of 'trust', 'Care', and 'love'.

'Filled with blooming flowers On both ends of the road.'

The clock 'Tiks' from second to minute, to years. "And things that depart

Friendship, instead strengthened and Evolved 'Protection'

'Nothing that reached the end Couldn't depart'

But~ "Created a true friendship

That shinned so bright, That nothing shone brighter."

Sujal parikh

Sujal Parikh hails from the Cultural city Vadodara also known as 'Sanskari Nagari'. He has been working with Savli Technology & Business Incubator as Technical Facilities Assistant for over 5 years supporting Biotechnology based innovative start-ups, in their journey from ground to sky. His educational qualification in field of Electronics & Communication Enginnering has prepared him with technological as well as commercial aspects of life. Some of his work could be addressed on Miraquill application (user id: sujalparikh). He especially enjoys writing thoughts and poems based on the life changing realities.

दोस्ती हुई ऐसी जिसका कोई मोल नहीं
परिवार मिला ऐसा जिसका कोई तोल नहीं

ज़िन्दगी हकीकत से ज़्यादा एक हसीं वाक़्यां बन जाती है, जब कभी तेरी याद जाने अनजाने मेरे पास चली आती है

तुम्हारे साथ से ही मिलते है हौसले; सही लगते है सारे लिए फैसले |

यूँ ही अपना साथ बनाये रखना; खुद से हमें मिलाये रखना |

अपने प्यार से ज़्यादा इश्क़ किया है तुम्हे; किस्मत ने ज़िन्दगी भर के साथ में बंधा है हमे |

भले ही हाथ तेरा मेरे हाथ में रहे न रहे, रोज़ यही याद करने की फ़रियाद रहे न रहे;

चाहे हम तुझसे अपने दिल की हर कश्मकश कहे न कहे, तेरे हर दर्द और तकलीफ को तेरे जितना सही न सही;

फिर भी हर पल हर एहसास से जुड़ा है तू; तेरी सारी मन्नते कबुल हो उसे, वही उम्रभर की मेरी दुआ है तू |

जितना तूने संभाला है उतना कोई न कर पायेगा; जब तक रहेगा तेरा साथ, ये हर बिगड़ी बात बनाएगा |

कभी अपनी ताकत का नहीं करूँगा घमंड, हार को भी जीत में बदल दू ईमान है उतना बुलंद ||

एक है दुनिया, एक हु में |

इस दुनिया में लोग अनेक;

उन् अनेक में ख़ास हे तू, मेरे दिल के पास हे तू |

तू ही दुनिया, तू ही दिल; चल कही आके चुपके से मिल |

तू है तो सब कुछ ख़ास, हर पल खुशियों संग मन हताश ||

UNPLANNED CHOICES ARE THE MOST HAPPENING ONES

Once d so called strangers are family now! When they r there nothing else is really required Believe me nothing's gonna stop me ever...

There are people who might misunderstand your talks or expressions but with friends it hardly matters because your souls are connected.

Even a bottle of whisky cannot intoxicate me enough, as much as I'm even with a glance of your picture.I don't need everybody to be a part of my life, I just need that few selected ones with whom I & with me they could live happily ever-after!

The sky has limits to expand, the river has boundaries to flow, the trees have age restrictions to grow, even d best has d adverse effects to affect... But trust me friends will be the only one's in your life whose love will never get older ~ rather it'll flourish infinitely.

Today I would just thank them all for making this togetherness Flawsome:

For sincerely accepting all that emotional drama and laughing out loud even at d worst of my jokes, for always solving my jumbled up situations, for continuously listening to my nonsense talks without having earplugs or putting in cotton swabs, supporting in small-big gimmicks, you are my lifeline's spare soul ~ sometimes I feel jealous of thoughts that if you got

got married and will prioritize me less but I would be more contended as you will have two gardeners to cherish your evergreen life. If anything is left apart I would leave it up to you because you are equally entitled with this relation.

एक अनोखा रिश्ता और उसके तौर-तरीके

ज़िन्दगी में कई तरहाँ के लोग मिले, कुछ हमदर्द मिले तो कुछ कमज़र्फ मिले;

ख़ुशी की बात ये है के तुमसे न हुए कभी कोई शिकवे गीले।

नाही हमने कभी किसी की जूठी तारीफ़ की,

नाही कभी उन्हें सच्ची शिकायत का मौका दिया।

दोस्ती रंग रूप की मोहताज नहीं,

इन्हे तो बस बेइन्तेहाँ प्यार और अटूट विश्वास से ही संभाला जा सकता है।

सुबह की गरमा गरम चाय से रात को सोने से पहले वाले ठन्डे दूध तक का साथ होते है ये दोस्त!

गुस्सा रहता है इनकी नाक पर और ज़िद्द को बना ले जो अपना हथियार,

दूसरे ही पल होठों पर मीठी बोली और बाहों में भरके करते है तुमसे प्यार।

हर कोई अपने आप में कोहिनूर सा है,

कभी दुर होकर भी पास और कभी पास होकर भी दुर सा है।

इन्हे कभी किसी की नज़र नहीं लगती,

ज़्यादातर वही पाए जाते है जहा दुर्घटना है घटती।

तुम परेशानी में देखकर हर मुसीबत से लड़ जाएंगे,

वरना देखो तो डरावनी पिक्चर में भी गभरायेंगे।

यारी चीज़ ही ऐसी है, चैन कभी ना लाएगी,

दोस्त सामने हो या दुर, ये ज़ालिम बेचैनियां ही बढ़ाएगी।

दोस्ती ने बस इतना सिखाया है मुझे, गुरु सोचना मत कभी बस हो जा शुरू; मित्रो के लिए जब भी करूं, तब खुदा से पहले दुआ करूं ||

SCHOOL-COLLEGE LIFE: WHERE YOU EARN THE MOST OF THEM

This was about the time when a huge tide of friends fluttured some stucked, others washed away. What mattered was their presence. Friends always support you in good and bad but a real friend will never allow you to get into trouble. They hang out with you, some gets close to your family and social life whereas some are just for upliftment your mood. Seniors, juniors, some with d similar age; all that matters is taste of habits and reverence of joy.

They are damn wonderful not becaue they wears gorgeous trendy attires or were propertied but it's the love they receive and emit naturally... Never demanding other than your time and care, always satisfied with whatsoever they are served with. Memories we shared together are wonderful. It wasn't & never ever will be a give and take relationship but yes an individual only earns and achieves when he/she eagerly unstoppabbly craves for it. Only love can be divided endlessly, and still not diminish. Here are some who gave everything up on you without remembering and where u also accepted that all without forgetting.

Though all our spent moments might not be as cheerful and happening as you supposed them to be but at last you are back together as never before...Though being the weirdest creatures, would always be grateful for selflessly reviving out d insanity from all over!

43

तेरी मेरी यारियां
सबसे ज़्यादा प्यारियाँ

ज़िन्दगी कैसी है पहेली, मिल गई तुझ जैसी एक सहेली;
तुमसे मिलती है एक प्यार भरी ख़ुशी, मिलते रहना हमेशा यूँही तुस्सी |

हमारे रिश्ते में भी क्या खूब गहराई है, एक ऐसी गुत्थी जो सुलझाए और उलझे;
कभी कटी पतंग की डोर सा खामोशियों में बिखरा हुआ, तो कभी मांझे से कसके लिपटा हुआ उसी पतंग को सखाए;
जैसा भी हो बड़ा ही रंग बे रंगी और ख़ुशनुमाह सा लगता है |

तुमसा ना मिल पायेगा, जिससे दिल संभल ये जाएगा;
फिर भी तेरे मुँह में घी शक्कर, अगर चल गया कही मेरा चक्कर;
थी न कभी होगी तेरी कोई टक्कर, ऊपर वाले ने भी बनाया है तुझे **बेइन्तेहाँ फुर्सत रखकर |**

कभी कुछ यु खूबसूरत एहसास दिलाते है वो, के खुद पर यकीन नहीं होता;
कभी इस कदर ज़लील करते है की खुद पर से यकीन उठ जाता है |

आपकी गलती में जो खुद को ज़िम्मेदार मानते हो और आपसे ज़्यादा जिसे उसे सुधारने की चिंता हो; वह आप नहीं आपकी जीवन रेखा के अंश है |

आप की ख़ुशी में जिनके मुख पर आपसे ज़्यादा आनंद हो, वह आप नहीं आपकी जीवन रेखा के अंश है |

आपके जीवन की हर एक मुसीबत में जो एक जूठ होकर आपका कवच बनकर लड़ते है; वह आप नहीं आपकी जीवन रेखा के अंश है |

आपके टूटे ख्वाबो में जो खुद बिखर जाते है और फिर जीने का जज़्बा देकर हरा भरा बनाते है; वह आप नहीं आपकी जीवन रेखा के अंश है |

अब ये अंश भले ही हमारी ज़िन्दगी में अलग अलग नामो से आता है, लेकिन कुदरत की महफ़िल में इन्हे दोस्त का नाम दिया जाता है | कभी मीठी रसमलाई से तो कभी चटखारे गोलगप्पो से, कभी कड़वे काढ़े से तो कभी खट्टे निम्बू से पर आपकी असली स्वस्थता का रहस्य तो यही है कोई च्यवनप्राश नहीं ||

Razia Munir Mujawar

She born and brought up in mumbai 25th May 1991. She lives in Mumbai. She has completed Bachelor's degree in Education and Masters in Commerce. She has 2 years of working experience in E-commerce back-office as Sr.Executive and 3 years of working experience in Teaching (Geography and Economics- from Grade 6 to 10). Currently working as E-commerce Auditor in Iksula Pvt Ltd E-commerce firm. She likes teaching it inspires her knowledge. Her favourite hobby is singing and now writing has add on..!

अजीब सा एक रिश्ता

अजीब सा है ये रिश्ता
न खून का, न कोई दूर का रिश्ता
इस रिश्ते का कोई मोल नहीं फिर भी लगता है अपनेपन सा,
फिर भी होती है एक आस
फिर भी होती है इनकी फिक्र
बदले में कुछ भी नहीं चाहती है,
चाहत होती है तो साथ निभाने की
निभाते हैं वफादारी से
यारों इसी का नाम है Yaari

याद है वो दिन

याद है वो स्कूल का पहला दिन
गैरों के बीच तूने ही तो हाथ बढ़ाया था दोस्ती का
याद है वो दिन जब हम अपना सब कुछ शेयर करते थे,
चाहे वो टिफिन हो या पेंसिल या बुक हो और या फिर टीचर
की पनिशमेंट,
स्कूल से कॉलेज तक कुछ भी नहीं बदला उमर ही बदली,
वक्त बदला मौसम बदला पर हम ना बदले,
आज भी वो दिन को याद करके लब मुस्कुरा उठते हैं,
दुआ है खुदा से हमारी दोस्ती का सिलसिला यूं ही चलता रहे
चलता ही रहे..!

कलम ना बयां करें तेरी मेरी यारी

शायद कोई ऐसा कलम ही नहीं
जो तेरी मेरी यारी को बयां कर सके
ए खुदा ये कैसा रिश्ता बनाया है तूने, मुझे नाज है जिस पर,
वक्त बेवक्त जब भी तेरी जरूरत हुई तब भी तुझे साथ पाया
अपने पास पाया,
ऐसा रिश्ता जिसमें हर रिश्ते की झलक है,
शायद इसीलिए बहुत खास है,
और क्या बयां करूं?
शायद कोई ऐसा कलम ही नहीं
जो तेरी मेरी यारी को बयां कर सके...!

आज तुझे क्या खास दूं?

आज कुछ तुझे दूं? तो क्या खास दूं?

क्या तुझ से भी ज्यादा कुछ खास है?

चल एक वादा दूं - वादा वफादारी का,

अनमोल है उसे क्या दूं,

चाहे दूर हो या पास, वादा है रहूं हमेशा तेरे साथ

आज कुछ तुझे दूं तो क्या दूं?

वादा वफादारी का वादा तेरे रूठने पर मनाने का

वादा तेरी हर बात को समझने का

वादा चाहे कितनी भी लड़ाई हो फिर से बात करने का वादा,

वादा तेरी हर बेवकूफी पर हंसने का और फिर मनाने का,

वादा तेरी हर गम और खुशी में साथ निभाने का

यह वादा है तुझसे चाहे जो भी हो

वादा निभाते चलेंगे वफादारी से...!

दिल-ए-बयान...!

आज कुछ बयां करूं इस रिश्ते को,

जैसा भी है खास है तू, परछाई सा पास है तू

दिल की डायरी में शामिल है तू,

बचपन से लेकर जवानी में शामिल है तू,

वक्त बेवक्त मेरे साथ है तु,

तेरे साथ वक्त बिताना अच्छा लगता है,

मेरे अश्क का हमदर्द है तू,

मेरी हर खुशी और गम का साथ है तू,

चाहे दिन हो या रात मेरी फोन की घंटी का जवाब देना तेरे लिए जरूरी है...

मेरी नाराजगी या गुस्से को समझने वाला है तू,

सच में क्या मैं इतना खास हूं?

शुक्रिया मुझे इतना खास बनाने के लिए...!

Tapasya Shah

Tapasya Shah belongs to the cultural city of Vadodara. She is currently a 12th grade science student with an interest of writing quotes and blogs. Some of her works can be addressed on her website  (tapasyashahblogs. com). She enjoys writing her thoughts on life and self-improvement. As an ambitious person, she has big dreams in her eyes and constantly strives to become better.

With an all time learning mindset, she looks forward to upcoming opportunities as well as challenges with a positive attitude.

TO THE CRAZY ONES

Regards to all those crazy ones;
Who chose me as a cutlet to their hamburger buns.
Sometimes they became my moms and made the conversations snappy;
Yet I owe them for whatever they did to make me happy!
Canteen escapes just to have round the clock gossip;
 Teacher chasing student's misleading concepts of friendship.
 Struggling with sports by getting ready-made class notes;
Year ends with a distinction having mentor's complimenting quotes.
You were never supreme nor of little importance;
Hence the only ones who were forever adjacent.
 Whosoever nourished us with gravely scoldings,
Turned out to be best human molding
Choosing a career always brings in a confusion;
The biggest fear is not settling up but accepting group diffusion
. Stress was always entangled with funky punch of relaxation;
Never step back and comply with upcoming adventures without elimination.
The journey starts with sharing pen, books and tiffin;

Ends forever with the last and foremost peek through coffin.

 A photograph could never capture the real life flavory;
Though holds you forever giving beautiful memory!
With all the tenderness, I write;
You made my life a delight!

ARE YOU YOUR BEST FRIEND?

Before making others your friends, first be your own friend. Criticize yourself on your mistakes, Appreciate when you do good, Ask questions and Assess yourself on a daily basis. Never stop talking to yourself. Love yourself more than anybody. Be your Best Friend!

WHO ARE YOUR FRIENDS?

Are all of your friends about the same age as you? Don't just have all your friends belonging to your age group. Make some friends that are 3-4 years older than you, some which are 3-4 years younger and some children.

Why ?

The former will help and prepare you for your future endeavors. You will be more mature and good at understanding and maintaining relationships with all kind of people. The second will help you in remaining broad and open minded. You will be always be 'cool' and can easily change yourself with changing times. The third will help you in bringing out your innovative, creative and innocent qualities. They will always set an example for you to be ethical and honest.

Make a habit to have discussions with all of them and then see how not only your perspective but your whole life changes for better.

FRIENDS FROM THE SAME BLOODLINE

Whenever one thinks of 'FRIENDS' we instantly visualize our best friend, school & college friends and colleagues. Why not our brothers and sisters!?

According to me they should be regarded as your first friends.

They may be your siblings or even your distant cousins. They are usually the one who 'harass' you, embarrass in front of others but at the same time they take stand for you, fight for you and protect you. They may tease you immensely but can't stand others teasing you. They are first one to provide any help necessary, it may be in terms of money, advice or just a helping hand.

They may not share 'food' with you but will definitely share knowledge. They may take all the things you have but won't take opportunities away from you. They give you best advice possible and always think good for you. They help in keeping you grounded by always finding some or the other 'fault' in you.

You both know each other the best. You are bound to protect each other. They understand you in a better way than anyone else because you both are in the same line of blood. Certain things like

family issues that you can't share with others, can truly be shared with them.

You can go out freely and carefree with them. There is no place for ego and the fear of hurting anyone. It does not matter How much you make fun of each other, no one is ever going to get upset. And even if one does, the other knows the cure for it. Anger does not last long between you.

All those snappy conversations and secrets you have with your 'friends' make the relation far more beautiful and enjoyable.

This is to all those friends of blood relation, Thank You So Much (for the first and last time)!

THOSE 21 DAYS

From the friendly matches & loving sessions,
To the fun on court & mannequin challenge.
From washing clothes at 1 am,
To eating out every alternate day.
From gossips every night at the garden,
To going out to malls every weekend.
From the annoying 'Hitler',
To morning 'oh ho ho' song.
Those short 21 days of camps
Gave me some of the best experiences!
 From sleeping in the programme 'bhashan',
To waking up early for yoga.
I thank everyone who have been a part of these,
And I feel sorry for those who missed
'Cause these are the happiest memories which you can carry throughout your life!
Hope you remember these

QUIET:

Just want to keep quiet,
And recall all the memories we have. Missing the moments shared with you, The memories that are made with you!
 Just want to sit beside you and gossip all day long,
Just Want to hug you tight and never let you go any long. Don't know why your absence is killing me from inside, Don't know when everything will be alright!
Missing the gossips we had every evening, Missing the walks that we use to take every night. Missing our silly fights,
Missing you from deep inside. Only one line meant for you, You are my life!
Without you i am half alive.

Inner Voice

Give me birth, i will make you feel proud. Grow me up,
i will never let you down.
Don't kill me,
You will only regret.
Allow me to see the world, Allow me to feel the pain,
Allow me to enjoy the happiness, Let me dream big
Let me acheive it, Let me fly high,
Let me touch the sky!.

A letter to self

I know you are not feeling right, It's like nothing left to fight!

So you have given up all your hopes!! As for life has nothing better to show. But dear, just hang on to this feeling, Consider it as it your needing.

This will make you wise,

And this is what you will need when you will rise! The day when you will finally taste your success, Trust me, it will be this life lesson you will cherish! With full of hopes to help another soul in distress!.

Journey of life

I ask you not to fear,

As you move through your life. Remember, i never left your side! Not everything in life goes smoothly,

Not everything in life will go as you have hoped! Soemtimes, its better to surrender your thoughts, On how you think, things should be!

And accept whatever you receive. This is how you create your LIFE! This is how LIFE creates YOU!.

Hope

Rising with a new hope again,
Thinking about somethgood might can happen. Waking up every morning and praying for it,
Tired of asking for the same thing again and again.
Hoping of getting it someday,
Hiping of achieving it oneday.
Don't have any assurance of getting it, But HEART doesn't want to believe it. Expectations are high,
Dreams are big,
Want to catch it oneday! And never let it go anyday!!.

Shabana Y. Solanki

She is Shabana Y. Solanki . her qualifications are BA first year from Amravati Arni , Dt . Yavatmal Maharashtra. She is a business woman. Her hobbies is writing and to work hard everyday.

बचपन की दोस्ती

बचपन था बहोत सुनहरा।
खेलते कुदते दिन बितता सारा।
दोस्ताना था इतना प्यारा।
दुख दर्द भुल जाते हम सारा।
बीते दिन की याद अब हमे सताये।
दिन बीते ना बीते बिताये।
दोस्त हमे इतने याद आये।
अब तक थे जिन्हे हम भुलाये।
दोस्त से ही है दोस्ती।
दोस्ती से ही है ज़िंदगी।
दोस्त ही करे हमारे
हर दुख की रवानगी।
दोस्त साथ हो तो,
हर मुश्किल आसान।
दोस्त बिना अधूरा है हर इन्सान।
रास्ते मे चाहे हो चट्टान।
दोस्त करे हर मुश्किल आसान।
आज सोचा तो आँसू भर आये।
मुद्दतें हो गयी मुस्कराये।
दोस्त तो हमनें बहोत थे बनाये।
मुद्दतें हो गयी उन्हे भुलाये।
ज़िंदगी हमे उलझन मे ऐसे उलझाये।
की बचपन के दोस्तो को हम भुलजाये।

आज सोचा तो आँसू भार आये।
मुद्दतें हो गयी मुस्कराये।
रिश्तेदारो के तो बहोत है साये।
पर दोस्त हमे हर पल याद आये।
आज सोचा तो आँसू भर आये।
मुद्दतें हो गयी मुस्कराये।
दिल के दरवाजे को जब हम खटखटाये।
तब सारे दोस्त हमे नज़र आये।
आज सोचा तो आँसू भर आये।
मुद्दते हो गयी मुस्कूराये।
ज़िम्मेदारीयो तले अरमान हम दबायें।
दोस्त और दोस्ती हम पीछे छोड़ आये।
आज सोचा तो आँसू भर आये।
मुद्दतें हो गयी मुस्कराये।
किस्मत ऐसा मोड़ ज़िंदगी मे अब लाये।
बिछड़े दोस्त सभी हमे मील जाये।
तो ज़िंदगी के सारे गम हम भुल जाये।
आज सोचा तो आँसू भर आये।
मुद्दतें हो गयी मुस्कराये।

सच्चा दोस्त

पंखो को पा लिया है मैने ।
पैरो की मुझको जरुरत नही ।
सच्चा दोस्त पा लिया है मैने ।
गैरो की मुझको जरुरत नही ।
उड़ान भरना सिख लिया है मैने ।
चलने की मुझको जरुरत नही ।
सच्चा दोस्त पा लिया है मैने ।
गैरो की मुझको जरुरत नही ।
खुदासे गुफ्तगू करती हू मैं ।
ज़माने की मुझको जरुरत नही ।
सच्चा दोस्त पा लिया है मैने ।
गैरो की मुझको जरुरत नही ।
संघर्ष को अपनालिया है मैने ।
सहारे की मुझको जरुरत नही ।
सच्चा दोस्त पा लिया है मैने ।
गैरो की मुझको जरुरत नही ।
जंग करना सिख लिया है मैने ।
भागने की मुझको जरुरत नही ।
सच्चा दोस्त पा लिया है मैने ।
गैरो की मुझको जरुरत नही ।

कोरोना से दोस्ती

अभी अभी देखा मैने एक सपना।
बर्थडे विश करने आये मुझे कोरोना।
कहा दोस्त गिफ्ट क्या चाहिये ये बोलोना।
कहा मैने उनसे की जनाब कोरोना।
आपसे सभी भयभीत हैना।
आप अगर चाहते हो मुझे गिफ्ट देना।
तो प्लीज यहासे दर चले जाओना।
हम सब इन्सानो को बख्श दो ना।
आप धरती मे समजाओना।
या आसमान मे चले जाओना।
कहा उन्होंने बड़े प्यार से
तथास्तू दोस्त शबाना।

अनजाना दोस्त

कोई हमे ज़िंदगी मे ऐसा खास मील जाये।
जिये हम ऐसे के मिसाल बन जाये।
बाद हमारे मौत के भी
चर्चे हमारे खास बन जाये।
जिये हम ऐसे के मिसाल बन जाये।
गम हमारे जिन्दगी से डर के भाग जाये।
सामना करे हम गमो का
ऐसा की मिसाल बन जाये।
जिये हम ऐसे के मिसाल बन जाये।
बिन कुछ कहे ही कोई ,
दोस्त हमे समझ जाये।
तब जिये हम ऐसे के मिसाल बन जाये।
पर किसिके भी समझ मे,
 ना हम अब तक आये।
तो भला कैसे जिये की,
मिसाल बन जाये।

Manjit Baishya

His name is Manjit Baishya and he is doing his degree in Guwahati University, Assam. He loves writing and have written a few poems and short stories. He writes randomly, there  is no specific bondage for his schedule and this is his first time attempting to publish it somewhere! Hope you like them.

THANKS

Empty days and empty nights, Don't know what reason it binds;

Things get better when done than said,

Work stuff out and don't be just a bait.

Reasons are plenty for you to quit, Farmers don't stop because of the heat; You don't whine, you do it anyway After the night, there comes a day!

Millions of hurdles there lay ahead We are to get tired before the bed; How can you say that your bed is good If you didn't even split some wood.

These were some things I was taught, Each time I lost a battle I just fought, They told me to move on,

Untill the pain I felt was gone!

Some things they said went right through me Coz they showed me things I was afraid to see, Thanking them would be the smallest deed

I hope this will bring a smile when you read!

FAMILY

There were five solos in my class, None saw one-other, they just pass;

Several days passed by, it went like that, Didn't know that, fate will hit us with bat!

Days passed by, we started talking, Spent time together, started walking, We started to know each other, Made sure, we didn't bother.

We were still threes and threes, Took it slow, so we didn't freeze; I knew we would bond very well,

Despite out differences, as a spell!

We finally came together, Forming a six, else, we didn't bother; What fate holds, hope to face together, Yet, feelings are soft, just like a feather!

I honestly love you all, You pick me up, when I fall, Unknowingly we became family, A love in me, surprisingly!

THE SHY GUY

Once came a boy and asked for a seat, Asked if it was free, and I said indeed;

Looked shy at first but then things changed Pages unfolded and they got arranged.

We blended quite good, to be true As former members of a crew, Stayed detached for some days Then connected in random ways.

We shared stuff, no one else knew, They didn't deserve to smell that brew, Caring for each other step by step,

I wrote this poem without any prep!

YOU

I stumble across even small pebbles, Cannot hear the song of the beetles; Somethings just break my heart right open, Then you come, right up, hold me frozen!

We know each other fair enough, Teaching each other how to be tough; Growing on the opposite sides of love, What we really have is far above!

We trust each other in all cases, Open our masks and show our faces,

We are like siblings but with no fights, Touching new heights with bright lights.

I feel blessed to have you by my side, Releasing me from the shackles of life, Never would have gone so far without you

I believe we were meant to meet out of blue!

Sudeshna Kundu

She is a reader, a wannabe artist, bagged a job last year in this IT sector and she loves writing motivational quotes. Also, a cat-lover and she wants to do something for abandoned street cats in the future. Someday she wishes to own a small library at her place.

HOSTEL DIARIES

"Bye, maa... I can manage", I tried to sound apathetic, as much as I could.

I actually wanted her to go...so that I could enjoy my most awaited independence .

She asked my would-be roomie to take care of me.

Yes, I'm the only child of over-possessive Bengali parents.

I love them but sometimes it is a bit over showering... but back then the only thing lingering was my concern for my freedom, explore a world outside the family that is, friends, and hostel.

It has been five years now.

It had been almost 18 years that I was staying with my parents when I barely had any restrictions on studying the subjects of my choice, eating, or befriending guys.

I had restrictions on gossiping with friends because that is not productive according to them...but talking about your crush with your best friend is productive to me.

I had restrictions on "not-studying" ..most obvious.

So the very thought of joining an engineering college, staying in a hostel was just a wave away.

As soon as my mom left, I shut the door and I felt happy.

Happy? Yes, because I was very very excited.

Raeesa and I talked till 2 am about my IIT-ian crush, she insisted me to send a follow request on Facebook, she was more serious about my crush than I was. She insisted that I can still carry on with my stalking skills... I guess I have taken that advice way too seriously. She had been my roommate for 4 years and my very first friend in college. After the first day, going off to bed at 3:00 a.m. became a new normal.

Also, I met Ms. Meenakshi Singh, it was not a best-friendship, at first sight, I tell you.

DISCLAIMER: HER BROTHER LOOKS REAL GOOD.

Well, this was the rumor.

Now her brother is happily married. And she is not my sister-in-law. So readers, don't get these false notions.

I made many friends later on in those 4 years. I started to value friendships more. We all had our own fights, our own struggles...even fights amongst each other. We all valued our tears... In the end, we became a small family. And also, complaining about shitty food was an unintended compulsive dining discussion.

Hostel had different restrictions in itself but living your life on your terms was a transition in adulting.

Not staying with my parents for 5 years now...made me love them more(I used to love them earlier

too), made me a bit more responsible in every aspect now.

It had now been almost three weeks of being a college student, attending classes that we all got tired of this schedule...being a junior is not an easy thing when you get drowned in assignments every other day.

"It's 8:05 a.m. already, it has been raining for the past 5 hours, how to go for classes?", my roomies sounded so concerned and I felt way too sleepier than ever. My roommates were up already and I was still tucked in a blanket.

Suddenly, our phones made the most awaited noise... messages from WhatsApp class group. The very thought of staying inside the hostel room getting tucked in blanket and sleeping was telepathic by the initiation of "MASS BUNK". The unofficial online class group was flooded with messages like "YouTube tutorials are the best, the syllabus can be dealt anyhow", "Weather is flirting with me", "My roomie promised to teach me that chapter, it is an easy one, we don't need a professor for that", "need study leaves!!" ," We have always had good attendance, one day leave should not matter"...etc.

Conclusion: MASS BUNK is a mismanaged concept, highly idealistic, it was unsuccessful by five per cent, all thanks to the very few students who had the urge to grasp the knowledge not on usual days but on the most unusual ones. I was still on the bed for the next four hours.

"Have you solved chapter 3 problem number 4?" Madhu, my roomie asked.

"Not yet, still on the second chapter", I replied. I remembered, prior to three weeks, someone said that

Youtube tutorials are a saviour. Well, it's true, it was 11:00 pm and there are four chapters, I am on my second and there is this exam tomorrow at 9:00 am with an assignment submission at 3:00 pm the next day. Well, half of the assignment was done and I donated that to my neighbouring room and the rest half I needed to copy from my another neighbouring room.

PS: Yes, I have an engineering certificate and we all have copied lab assignments mostly.

That was sorted though...but the saviour videos of YouTube went till 4:00 am accompanied with two bowls noodles and a sleep-deprived mind. But the energy you have on the day before the exam is beyond explanation. Next day, I had this exam for two hours and to tell the truth... I was damn sleepy after submitting my answer scripts but there was some voice," what option did you select for the first question, and was the answer for this question..." and I immediately interrupted him and said "I'm in a

hurry, I have to submit an assignment" instead of replying "you can actually run after the invigilator, it's not that late though and you can see my answer script for that".

I have some serious issues with comebacks.

Later that night inside my hostel room, when I was actually supposed to doze off to sleep after a long day, I preferred watching movies with my friends with some pizza.

B.Tech certificate not only fetched me a job , it fetched me friends, made me have the best family outside my own home. From exams to getting a job everything happened because of my friends. I will cherish all my memories with them forever.

Josephi joshni. S

She is Joshni from Kanyakumari, Tamil nadu. Writing poems is just not her passion it's her tool to burst her stress and writing poems helps her to travel beautiful world apart from this life.We can create our own world during writing and being a  English student it helps her to play with vocabularies like singing with birds. It's quiet fun.

Life sang a song

Saying something wrong
I invoked my God
There entered my friends
I'm surprised it's God who sent
I'm a moon
With emotions of tune
No one could realise me soon
At my first they were rude
I never thought they will become my dude
We become so close
By people we choose
People like them rare
With concern and care
Time waiting for bus
Chemistry lab we rush

Our unrevealed secret
And chemistry lab burette
Those astonishing memories
Leap in my dreams
Time we spent
And the school we went
Made us closer ever my friend
My mental wars and painful scars
Taken away by these stars

My unlimited stories Only they could hear
If they couldn't mind me I couldn't bear
The way they care and always share
Makes them my angels
I swear
I never said them bye
Still their bliss in my eye
One became doctor The other engineer
Another became English poet
All are unique rather
Their eyes always attracts
Their hands warmly protects
Love for me refracts
If the day is hotter
Slashing cool water
Extreme celebration makes
Face full of cakes
Passing test papers
Tasting colorful wafers
Each day is special
Absence of racial
One hour talk
All my Stress unlocks
Mocking at our crushes
Being priceless treasure
Though there are enemies

My friends help like honey bees
Day till today
They pass my way
Maybe in one's marriage
We all gonna meet
I wanna big storage
So that I could seat
Funs we made
That never fade
They are Angels of God
Protects me from swords
When situation worst
They help their best
All I want a therapy
They want to be my nearby
Our beautiful smiles
Says a tale
Days we spent
Sings song till end
From six to now
They were my dove
Never leaves me
I wonder how?
Days spend together
Asks us to gather
Until we meet again

Sing and enjoy the rain
Their love for me
Compares the sky
With them I'm a butterfly
They make moments glitterfly
Love is so thin
Only friendship could win
Although they were apart
My soul yearns a lot
"We may go far and far
But treat me stranger lol".

Dr Smita Anand Sriwastav

She is a gynaecologist by profession and a poet at heart. She is currently residing in Varanasi. She has been writing poems since she was in high school and plan to do so forever. Nature is a driving force that inspires her poetry and she tends to find poetry in the ordinary things. My blog where she posts often is Rainchimes Poetry by Smitaanand www.drsmitasriwas280.wordpress.com

You Me and Cappuccino...

Tasting an amateur cappuccino
drooled by
my prodigal coffee maker
from chipped porcelain cups
with you, on evenings abuzz with strains
of crickets drunk on tequila dusks,
is better that drinking red wine
from sultry brandy balloons
in a restaurant echoing
with soft violin music and laughter
because we together share
a platonic love affair,
we both love coffee and we
are both teetotallers

Noodles

from our ancient frying pan,
taste better than hors d'oeuvres
invented by a master chef,
that pickled in green chillies,
sprinkled in spices,
and laced in lemon juice,
for we are obsessed with Chinese food
 noodles are like good friendship
spicy and savory,
we eat it from gaudy plastic plates
gossiping through
mouthsful of noodles,
our laughter
the exuberance to fill in baskets
of treasured memories.

Nostalgia

Hopscotching
on cobblestones
punctuated in grass blades,
in butterscotch sunshine,
rain drizzling like butterfly kisses,
shooting marbles
in the dirt strewn in autumn foliage,
and playing hide and seek
behind shrubbery haunted
by carnivorous mosquitoes,
we filled our pockets
with photons sweated by sun
on orangade skies at dusk,
salving skinned knees
with moonlight
eyes eager to race the allure
f fireflies in salsa.

Mornings

tasted insipid as cold cereal,
that gobbled down
under stern maternal glare,
except on sundays
when the noon sun cajoled
sleepy eyes like a benevolent grandpa
and we feasted on specials
from mom's kitchen,
burdened by backpack monstrosity
we shared tales
of classroom escapades,
crowded in the crotchety school bus
to make our scholarly pilgrimage.

Giant wheels

whirled a riot on tinseled evenings,
laughter and cries mingling
with aromatic syllables
of spicy popcorns and peanuts,
giggling on sea saws
and screaming in the saddle
of merry go round horses,
together we forged a strong bond
together living
a fairytale childhood gilded in bliss.

We wore

chocolate milk moustaches,
and candyfloss whiskers,
sharing coke bottles and icecream
tiffin time
was a potpourri of dishes
chocolates shared, bartered, begged
homework was joint effort
and often copy pasted
while exams dawned shivering
with apprehensive fear.

Days like frangipanis

and sweet sour blackberry nights
innocent promises
and petty woes were fodder f
or treacle smeared memories,
rain dances, paper boats sailed
in monsoon gutters,
mangoes were gathered
and butterflies collected in bottles,
marbles were like pearls
and kites a treasure.

Togetherness

blossomed in straits of childhood
with forever friendships
born like amaranthine dream,
playing, laughing, crying, singing
we defined dictums
of the first innocent friendship...

Friends are like Flowers...

A rose
she is beautiful
dainty and fragile, scenting
lives with inherent sweetness,
she paints rainbows
with her smiles on tempest clouds,
but wilts under
the deluge of angst.
She is
an amaranth
stoic, sturdy and enduring,
she is dauntless
with patience,
always facing storms
and surviving as the fittest.
A hursingar
she blooms under moonlight
drinking in lunar chardonnay
she is shy and secretive,
her insomnia
forever befriending
lonely nights that refuse
to slumber.
Gauche and simple
a marigold in bloom, she is clueless
unaware of affectation,
she is genuine

as her golden corolla,
dependable in rain and sunshine.
A lily she defines purity
always honest to a fault
she remains the nagging conscience
on your social horizon,
she mirrors your faults and refuses
to be deceptive.
A violet
she is decadent and mystical,
secrets bloom in her laughter,
she is a mystery,
seeking to be unraveled
making life interesting
and alluring with
her air of ambiguity.
Frivolous
is she as a cherry blossom
her moods quicksilver, t
ransient is her resolution,
dieting on cupcakes and exercising
on armchairs,
she is a breath
of fresh air always ready to
spice up the serious...

Vignettes of Friendship...

Sentences
completed and pauses read,
discerning
the angst draped by
bright brittle laughter,
gossips shared and fantasies aired
on afternoons flavoured
in chicken nuggets and cappuccinos.
Awful movies and boring lectures
endured with glee,
sharing secret jokes
with vociferous gazes and naughty grins,
teasing anecdotes
dogeared by persistent reminiscences,
long nights cuddled in
giggles and confidences.
Meals concocted, shared, botched
and tall tales exchanged,
shopping sprees and rickshaw rides,
petty quarrels and patch ups
pakoras dunked in ketchup.
Walks in the drizzling rains
sharing an umbrella,
corn on the cob tangy with lemon
and ginger tea in winter.
Pajama parties, night outs

cramming before exams till dawn,
bunking lectures and proxied attendance
imitating teachers for fun.
An amalgam of emotions
running riot,
bonds created with trust and love
pinky promises and blood vows
secrets sealed forever...

Sagas of Friendship...

Like a septet of variegated ribbons,
braided into a looming rainbow;
forged as a cord of friendship
between the distant clouds,
weeping tempest from
mascara lined eyes;
and the parched throat
of sweltering bosom, of earth.
As the kisses exchanged,
by dappled butterflies,
and redolent dewy roses;
that sticks to oblivious feet,
as ornate, auspicious
turmeric henna, of pollens
from scented core,
to build a new friendship.
Moths dancing in sinuous orbits,
around street lights;
with a lunar dream incandescent,
in hypnotized eyes of frenzy;
while an unknown, oblivious moon
sulks in loneliness of night's glens,
behind veils of ebon clouds;
are like distant strangers,
with friendship about to happen.

Serpentine railway tracks,
running side by side, on earth
never destined to embrace,
in amiable caress of friendship;
have harsh pebbles and stones,
that forge a union between them...

Bshayar52 is a community which provides his/her writers, an unimaginable platform. Every writer has a dream to publish his/her works one day and keep his book of thoughts open, in front of the world. Bshayar52 is that one community that aims to fulfil such unimaginable dreams of such writers. It aims to provide the writers, the best opportunity possible! "EACH PERSON HAS HIS OWN STORY, SORROW OR GLORY' similarly each writer has 'something' to say to the world; something it needs to change with his pen! This community provides the golden chance to raise their voices, without any fear of being told to shut up! I am proud to be a part of such a community which is growing day by day, dreaming to fulfil others' dreams Bshayar52 is not only a community; it's a family with great responsibility. It's connected with deep emotion; we are dedicated towards it with strong devotion. It's the finest milestones which lead us towards success. It encourages us to explore our feelings without any stress or worries about being judged by people. We also provide knowledge and training to present your emotions and how to publish it. We are here to increase your worthiness by organizing daily weekly and monthly challenges.

Writers with us and make your image globally. We as a team are very greedy, greedy for talent, talented writers. For us our team is everything and we as a team try to search every nook and corner for that one writer who would swell us with pride. We are not afraid of the penance. We await the beautiful pieces. We accept every writer amateur or professional; we are here for the writing community.